The Stories of Sister Sarah

Crossed

David Clark

1

The morning chill of the clear spring morning was now a thing of the past. Clear skies and a strong sun chased it away. It wasn't hot outside. It was pleasant, and a gentle breeze brought in a refreshing respite along with the sweet smell of jasmine and honeysuckle from time to time. There was no questioning why Sister Sarah called this her Eden, it truly was heaven on Earth.

Kenneth may have somewhat disagreed, as he had to search around for the perfect angle to set up to avoid having sunspots and glare during his shot. He tried to work around where the Sister sat, not wanting to ask the elderly nun to move. Though she did shift a little on the bench as he moved around. Ralph assisted by standing in a spot and then calling for Kenneth to bring the camera over there and check. Neither hesitated when Sister Sarah Meyer recommended taking today's sessions outside. It was beautiful and would provide an alternative to the dark wood and stone backdrops they have used over the last few sessions.

After a few moments of searching, Kenneth found the perfect spot and quickly setup. Ralph positioned the footstool he had carried outside with him in front of Sarah. Behind her, as always was one of her escorts, and her brother, Jacob.

"You were right. This is beautiful," Ralph said, motioning at the tree filled courtyard that was all around them.

"It is. This is my sanctuary. No matter what is going on, or how I feel, this is where I come to feel right as rain," Sarah said with a smile. "So, what shall we talk about today?"

"Well," Ralph started. "I was thinking we could talk about the hill."

"Lithuania?", Sarah tersely asked.

"If that is okay?"

Sarah looked around the courtyard and up into the olive tree leaves that blew in the breeze. It appeared she searched for a divine answer. Whether it arrived or not, only Sarah knew. She looked down at her hands in her lap and then up at her brother. There was a single tear dripping down her cheek.

"Sister, we can cover something else today," Ralph said as Jacob handed his sister a handkerchief.

"No, it's okay," she sniffed. "I knew we were going to have to talk about it at some point."

"We can wait," Ralph offered.

Jacob chimed in, "Maybe it is best if we wait."

"No. No. The story has to be told. There is no avoiding it. Let's go ahead." Sarah righted herself and handed the handkerchief back to her brother. She was again the picture of strong, resolute faith. "So, the hill in Lithuania?"

"Yes, Sister. That was what, eight years after you arrived here?"

"Eleven that October," corrected Sarah with a little smirk.

Ralph made a note on his notepad. "A few questions before we get started with what happened."

Sarah nodded her agreement.

"Before Father Lucian came to you, had you heard about the hill?", asked Ralph. He looked on eagerly for her response.

"No. I had never heard of such a place until that day. Since then, I have spent many hours reading up on it. On the surface, it is a fascinating place. A hill, with thousands upon thousands of crosses on it. Quite a sight from the pictures I have seen, and another good example of how the Church is able to control the story. For over a hundred years, everyone knew it as a monument for the struggles of the Lithuania people and the oppression they felt during the World Wars. Which, as we all know now, is somewhat true, but it has nothing to do with either World War I or World War II"

"And, Sister, what was the real purpose?"

"Mind you, a Pope even visited the site to further the hoax," Sarah said with a point and a chuckle.

"The real purpose?", Ralph asked again.

The chuckle and smile vacated Sarah, and she leaned forward with a sternness in her eyes. "It was a spiritual lock to contain a monster, of course."

"Are there any others like it around the world?"

"Of course," Sister Sarah said very matter-of-factly. "But don't ask me where because I won't tell you. Those things need to stay undisturbed." Her head shook from side to side, and she leaned back and crossed her arms.

"Of course not, Sister. I was just curious."

"Oh, I know. Most are, and I do get a sense from you and young Kenneth that neither of you are looking to cause any trouble." This was something Sarah realized about them during her first meeting and knew Jacob had as well, or Jacob would have never agreed to allow them to meet with her. "There is a lot more to this world than meets the eye. Hidden secrets, treasures, and truths all over the place. Take my word for it," she leaned forward and whispered, "everything is better if those stay hidden." Sarah studied Ralph, waiting for him to acknowledge her suggestion. When he did, she added, "We don't need you going out and doing any documentaries on those and have someone who doesn't know any better poking around and unleashing hell on Earth. There are enough of those that should know better doing that as it is, and I and my brother are way too old to fix things."

Next to her, Jacob puffed out his chest a little and drew a wry laugh from his sister. "I am younger than you, remember?"

"Oh, I remember. You are younger than me, but neither of us are spring chickens." She reached over and ran her fingers through his mop of grey hair, which Jacob did the same to straighten anything she had moved out of place. "This younger generation of keepers is a fine bunch and will do all right when dealing with the normal day to day, but there isn't a leader yet. Someone that will step forward when a real challenge appears, not like my brother here." Sarah was proud of her brother, probably more than she had ever really told him. It was part of the sister brother dynamic. She knew they loved each other, and she was immensely proud of him, even though she didn't say it as often as she should have or if ever. This was one of the first times she had ever vocalized it, and it appeared to embarrass Jacob as he broke eye contact with his sister. Similarly, Sarah knew Jacob was proud of her. Sarah kept her loving gaze on her brother.

"I am sorry, dear. I didn't mean to interrupt your questions. Continue," she said, turning back to Ralph.

"No apology needed," Ralph said. "The last question I have before we let you tell us about your experience at the hill, had you met Madame Styvia or Lord Negiev before you arrived in Lithuania?"

"Yes and no. Do I remember meeting them? No. But, they were part of the group of keepers that rescued me in Miller's Crossing and before I came here, which made things interesting. Let me go ahead and tell you my story, you will understand then."

A grouping of dark clouds formed above them, ruining the perfectly clear blue sky, and the refreshing breeze became evil.

2

"Dad, I am so sorry," Sarah said. She looked out from the woods as her father, Father Murray, Jacob, Father Lucian, and six strangers approached. Her father couldn't hear her at this distance. But, even if he were closer, he still wouldn't. She was there, but not. She could see the destruction she had caused, but IT wouldn't let her do anything about it except suffer the pure fear and despair that coursed through every fiber of her being like the water of all the worlds' rivers flowing through a garden hose at the same time. There was no way for her to stem the tide of sorrow. Suffer it she must, and death appeared to be her only salvation.

Four rapid knocks at her chamber door interrupted this all too familiar dream. Unfortunately, this interruption didn't happen far too often enough. When she thought about it in the first moments of cognitive thought as sleep lost its grasp on her, while the terror of the nightmare hung on, they had never woken her during the night in the eleven years since her arrival at the Abbey.

She sat up and looked around the room. Her quaint chambers should be completely dark while she slept; that was how Sarah would prefer it. The presence of her nightly tenders made her feel odd about it though, so she always kept a single candle lit on her nightstand. She swung her feet to the floor and oriented herself in the flickering light. It was silent except for the prayer that was a constant companion. It was something that was so much a part of her world it blended into her own existence to the point of not noticing it at all. A few times that caused her to panic and search for that sweet sound, just to make sure it was still there. For just a moment, she wondered if she had heard the knock in her dreams only, and looked at Sister Mary Theresa and asked, "Was there a knock?" The Sister didn't open her eyes when she nodded her head, confirming that the knock had indeed happened. If that wasn't enough of a confirmation, the second set of four rapid knocks was.

The stone floor was cold on Sarah's feet as she walked toward the door. Another round of knocking started, and she opened it between the second and third rap. On the other side was Father Lucian, out of breath and with a concerned look on his face she had never seen before. She didn't even see this much concern when he faced her down in her nightmare.

"Sister," he said with a gasp. "I need you to get dressed and come with me. Right now!"

"Father, what's going on?" Mother Francine asked. She rushed down the hall from her chamber. It was good, she asked. If she hadn't, it would be the next sound that escaped Sarah's mouth.

"It's Šiauliai. There's been an earthquake," he said.

Sarah didn't understand what he was talking about, but it was obvious her Mother Superior did. She stopped dead in her tracks and her hand leapt to her chest. "The seal... is it breached?", she asked.

"Holding, but barely. Everything fell."

Mother Francine rushed past Father Lucian and pushed past Sarah and into her room. "Child, let me help you get ready." Her hand grabbed Sarah's and pulled her inside. Sarah felt a tremble in her touch until she released her to close the door.

"Mother, what is it?"

"We must hurry," she said, and opened the simple bureau and pulled out a habit and placed it on Sarah's bed. "Come Sarah, you must get dressed." She turned to Sister Mary Theresa, who looked on from the corner, but never stopped her prayer. "Sisters Cecilia, Angelica and Genevieve will accompany her. Go get them prepared. I'll handle things here." Sister Mary Theresa stopped, stood up, and walked quickly to the door, and out. Mother Francine took up the position in the corner and began the prayer while Sarah got dressed.

"Mother, what is this place?", Sarah asked, and then attempted to repeat the name of the place she heard Father Lucian say, "Šiauliai?"

Mother Francine shook her head while she continued the prayer, but the look in her eyes said it all. She was scared. When Sarah finished getting dressed, she opened the door. Father Lucian was still outside. Without a word he started down the hall, and Mother Francine joined the pair in the hall and followed them out to the front.

"Father, can you tell me what is going on?", beseeched Sarah.

"Let's get to the car first," he said from the front of the line.

Sarah's escorts were waiting for them outside the front gate. They started praying as soon as she stepped through the gate. Mother Francine stopped. Father Lucian opened the front and back doors of the black SUV that waited for them. Her three escorts stepped into the back, and Father Lucian in the front, as was the normal seating order for all of her excursions out. Just as Sarah went to take her customary window seat in the back, Mother Francine grabbed her and pulled in close for an embrace that was tighter than normal. Quivers spread from her to Sarah, and her voice shook as she told her. "Take care, child. I mean it, be careful." She released her, which was more Sarah pulling away from her as Father Lucian urged her to hurry in. Sarah took her seat and closed the door as the vehicle sped off pressing her into her seat as she struggled to fasten her seat belt.

"Father, will you tell me what is going on?", Sarah asked.

He didn't turn around to look at her. He didn't even turn slightly in her direction. Instead, he stayed rigidly straight, eyes front, as he spoke. "At 10:13 pm local time last night a magnitude 7.2 earthquake hit Lithuania. Its epicenter was about fifteen miles from the small village of Šiauliai. The loss of life is already devastating, but it is nothing like what will occur if we don't intervene."

"There are aid organizations for this. The Red Cross and Red Crescent deal with these kinds of events all the time. What can we do?", Sarah asked. She didn't have a problem going to assist, but had to wonder what the urgency was for their small party to get in motion when thousands upon thousands of disaster aid trained volunteers would already be on the ground by the time they arrived, and why just them? If they were going to help, perhaps the whole convent should go. This didn't feel like one of their normal assignments.

"Sarah," he said and finally turned toward her. "Do you remember what I taught you about seals?"

This was a topic she had to think about to recall. The term was there in her head, but she hadn't heard it since then. It was mixed in with the symbolism of certain signs that one might come across and their meaning beyond what the public believes it to be. Some are warnings to stay away from places or objects, and others are locks meant to keep something sealed deep inside. One lesson came to mind. A picture of a simple tarnished brass doorknob with the cross and papal crossed keys on it. It was pretty, and one someone might picture being on a thousand or more year old door lining the hallways of the Vatican itself. Instead, it was on the door of an old Christian mission in Uganda. Behind the door, was a creature that possessed an entire village, turning its inhabitants against each other until it left no one alive. "The symbols?", she asked.

"Yes. The village of Šiauliai is the location of a hill with a seal on it. Underneath that hill is Ala, the demon of bad weather. But, don't let that name fool you. Yes, when it was loose it sent terrible weather, hail and tornados through crops and farms robbing an entire village of their food supply, starving them. That was just the edge of its power. When it wanted to really demonstrate true power and enslave people, it rained fire down on them, burning everything alive. In 1853 Pope Pius IX spent ninety-four days battling the beast before locking it in a deep hole beneath the ground. When the beast fell into that chasm it pulled the sides down on top of it covering it with earth. Pope Sylvester put a seal on top of the hill it created to lock it inside. The seal was a simple wooden cross planted into the ground. While it may seem small, it was powerful enough to imprison Ala. Through the years, thousands of pilgrims that understand the true meaning of the hill have placed additional ones adding to the security of the seal. Today there are over ten thousand crosses there. The earthquake knocked them all down, weakening the seal. I received a call from the keeper assigned there to watch over the seal that the ground was pulsing."

"Pulsing, Father?", Sarah asked. In her mind was the image of a bump of green grass rising and falling, like it was breathing.

He turned around further and looked Sarah right in the eye. "It knows the seal is gone and it is trying to get out."

3

The first light of the new day should have broken over the eastern horizon over an hour ago, but it hadn't. It was still pitch black as they drove into Šiauliai. The sun hadn't forgotten to come up that day. Sarah had seen it from the window of the plane, but it disappeared as they descended into a bank of what she believed to be clouds. They were clouds, but not of a natural variety. These were large rolling dark clouds of smoke and dust from the hundreds of fires burning across the countryside. Some probably fueled by broken gas lines caused by the earthquake, but an uneasiness creeping up her spine told her some were caused by something unnatural.

As they drove into the city, the glow from some of the larger fires helped illuminate the billowing clouds of smoke and back lit the piles of rubble that used to be buildings, business, and homes. The devastation was complete, and groups of people wandered around aimlessly, with their attention elsewhere, while members of the military and emergency services attempted to provide aid wherever they could. The car carrying Father Lucian, Sister Sarah, and her escorts didn't stop. Their destination was northeast of the city which was the direction everyone she had seen was looking.

Father Lucian had instructed the driver to take them to the Hill of Crosses Information Center, a tourist center for the location. It seemed the hill was such an oddity it had become a destination for tourists, which was not all that surprising to Sarah. Knowing there was a place you could go to see the world's largest ball of twine back in the States was proof that they could make any location into a tourist trap. Probably like all places, there would be a place to park, a building with artifacts and displays about the hill, and of course, a gift shop.

The car screeched to a sudden stop when Father Lucian cried out, "Stop right here! Right here!" They were in the middle of nowhere, with no information center in sight, meaning Sarah would have to wait to see if her assumptions were correct.

He opened the door and got out without a word to anyone. Sarah sat inside it and stared out at the foreign landscape from the safety of the car window. If she didn't know better, she would have thought Father Lucian had just brought them to a battlefield of some war between superpowers. Trees laid down all along the road, and in the distance a fire roared. The intensity of it seemed to grow and wane as each rumble below the car hit and disappeared. Sarah hadn't noticed the aftershocks when they were driving, but now that they sat still, the car rocked and rolled on its springs with every rumble.

After the third rumble, Sarah exited the car to search for Father Lucian who had disappeared into the darkness. He hadn't gone far and was just up the road from the car talking to someone. A woman who turned abruptly and scowled when she saw Sarah.

"Father! Why did you bring.. that... that abomination?", said the woman in a thick and harsh eastern European accent that cut at Sarah. The pale skinned woman with flowing raven hair took up an aggressive pose. Almost a crouch, as if ready to spring on a prey that crossed her path, and Sarah felt like that prey. "Don't we have enough to deal with?", she hissed.

Inside, Sarah felt something rumble and twist. This was the first time in years she had felt its presence when she hadn't tapped into it directly. The feeling of fear she felt multiplied, but her flight instinct wasn't close to being triggered. It was her fight instinct that was loading up, and it wasn't all her. It was mostly IT, and she couldn't quell it.

A hand from behind reached up and grabbed her wrist. Sarah looked down at the hand and followed the arm back to Sister Genevieve, who stood close and prayed. The dark brown eyes of the mid-thirties French nun, who had become a close friend of Sarah's, begged her, and Sarah didn't have to ask what it was about. They could all feel IT stirring inside her. She prayed herself and closed her eyes, attempting to calm everything down. She felt it was working until she felt a breath on her face. She opened her eyes and found herself face to face with the woman.

"Father, get her out of here. Now!", said the woman as she stormed off. "I should have killed her when I had the chance. You said you would keep her under control. This is not under control. I feel it inside her, wanting to get out. Wanting to do what IT does best. And she," she said while her arm exploded behind her with a point back at Sarah, "can't stop it if it wants to."

"She has far more control than you give her credit for. Plus, she has help. And, she is our best hope for solving this problem," said Father Lucian.

"Psh. I seriously doubt that," she scoffed.

It added to the buildup Sarah felt growing inside. This time it wasn't her companion, Abaddon, not that she knew of. This was all her. Her pride and stubborn attitude, both she had to fight at times to keep in check at the convent. Here they were about to be on full display.

"Excuse me, but who the hell are you?," Sarah asked as she chased the woman. "I am in complete control of whatever you think I am."

Sarah had barely finished her declaration before the woman turned and leapt at her, covering an unimaginable distance for a human. Her hand gripped around Sarah's throat and lifted her up with a strength that didn't match her feminine frame. "Let's see how much control it allows you to keep while I choke the life out of you."

"Styvia, put her down. Now!", Father Lucian yelled, and he put himself in between the two women. "Now stop it. We are here to deal with that!", he pointed in the hill's direction to remind them as the ground beneath their feet rumbled again.

"Yes, Father," the woman said.

"Sarah, you will need to excuse Madame Styvia. You two have met once. She was one of the keepers that risked her life to rescue you," Father Lucian said to Sarah, and then turned his attention to Madame Styvia. "Styvia, control yourself. If you feel Abaddon, it is not because of Sarah's lack of control. It is because of the proximity of it to Ala. They are from the same hierarchy of demons. She has complete control over it, and the sisters that are here with her are the safety net just in case."

Styvia? The name was strangely familiar to Sarah, but couldn't remember specifics. She didn't remember seeing her before, even though she had just been told she had. How could she not remember seeing a woman that looks like the bride of a vampire himself with her dark hair, and pale white skin? A sadness she hadn't felt in years came back to her. Sarah knew people had been hurt and killed by what had happened. Had she hurt this woman? Maybe she killed someone she loved or knew? That would explain her reaction. This dark scar on Sarah's past was one she tried to cover up with all the good she had done, but no matter what, it always resurfaced and took a toll on her spirit.

"Now, tell me the current situation?", Father Lucian asked Madame Styvia. Behind them was a gathered mass of townsfolk who were not worried about cleaning up the damage done to their town. Instead, they were concerned about what was occurring on the hill.

"The seal is cracked, not broken, yet. But, I can't tell how bad the crack is. I can't get close enough," Madame Styvia reported.

"Why not?", Father Lucian asked and stepped toward the hill himself. The strongest rumble of the ground rolled past them, throwing the car up in the air and into a ditch next to the road. Sarah and her escort landed sprawled out on the tarmac of the road. Father Lucian tumbled and landed on his backside on the road. Madame Styvia had crouched low to the ground and rode the wave.

"That's why," she said.

As the rumble cleared past them, Sarah felt a familiar tingle and a dark and cold presence off in the distance. She had barely felt it on the drive in, but there was no mistaken it was there now, and it was an evil that weighed down on both her body and soul. It pulsated with the glow from the fire on the hill.

"Either it is another quake, a ring of fire that chases us back, or the attacks on your mind. And now, there is some force... just there," she pointed in front of her," I can't get through it. I am trying to do what I can from here to seal any cracks," continued Madame Styvia.

Sarah got up to her feet and took a few steps forward, beyond Father Lucian and Madame Styvia. She held her right hand out and extended both fingers into an area of unseen power at the edge of her reach. It pushed back at her, but Sarah's fingers pierced the barrier for just a moment before it pushed back, sending her tumbling down to her backside. Her hand and arm tingled painfully. "I can feel it."

4

"I can too, and even you can't get through," mocked Madame Styvia. "We need to do something fast, and I am not thrilled about doing this in the dark."

Father Lucian strode back to the car and leaned in the passenger seat. From where Sarah stood, she could see he was plundering through his bag. He emerged wearing a red stole, and a familiar crown of thorns. She saw the bible in his hands as he walked past her, and without a word stepped into and through the barrier that had just repulsed her backward to the ground.

"Let's go," he said. His words muffled by a rumble that seemed more like the growl of some great beast below their feet. Even when the peak of the rumble subsided, there was a slight low vibration, re-enforcing the image of a great beast letting out a growl with every exhale. The ground moved up and down just enough to be felt with every sound.

Madame Styvia fell in behind Father Lucian. Both crossed through the barrier with ease. They paused on the other side and waited on Sarah. It was now her turn. Of course, it wouldn't just be her. Sisters Genevieve, Angelica, and Cecelia would need to accompany her in. She felt a dread, not for what was ahead of her, but for what the others were about to go through. She felt the dark and deep hatred of evil that waited at the hill for them. It was there in the air, in the dust, and in everything else around them. Infecting everything and everyone around, sending them further into despair.

"It will be okay," she said to the other sisters, trying to sound like an expert who knew exactly what would happen. Inside, she had no clue what they were all in for other than it wasn't good.

They didn't hesitate or waver. Just as always, the Sisters of San Francisco did their duty and stepped through in a line, one after another. Praying the entire way. Only Sister Genevieve looked up at Sarah as she passed. She was the one sister Sarah had connected with the most since her arrival. They crossed through and joined Father Lucian and Madame Styvia without incident. It was now Sarah's turn.

She had tested the barrier once and pushed into it. Whatever 'it' was, it didn't seem to like her intrusion and threw her back. What it would do now, she didn't know. Had Father Lucian cleared a path? It appeared he had. The others had no problem walking through. She didn't know for sure, but had to trust her faith. Both her faith in Father Lucian, and her own faith.

Each step was timid as she crossed through. There was nothing as she followed the same path as the others. Always being a curious animal, she reached to the side with her left hand and leaned. It was there, just a few feet away. She yanked her hand back as soon as she felt it. Any desire of a repeat of earlier had left her, and she stayed on the straight and narrow path Father Lucian had cleared for her. Much like she had for the last several years.

They walked in single file passed the mangled downed trees, and large patches of Earth thrusted up. Whether they had been done so by natural forces or supernatural, Sarah wasn't sure. It didn't really matter. The entire scene was a display of massive destructive power. She had never seen the area before, but with a village so close she had to imagine it was a beautiful countryside, and not the dystopian scene from one of the lower levels of Hell it was now. It was made even more so with the glowing of fires along the horizon everywhere you looked. The one ahead of them glowed brighter than all the others. The dark red halo grew with every rumble of the ground.

They walked for several minutes toward the hill, with the ground rumbling under their feet. Sarah felt a stomach pain developing. It wasn't much at first. Just the typical pain she had a few times as a child when she ate too much, or had something that didn't agree with her like the time her father tried an Asian recipe he saw on television. She visited the bathroom more than her own bedroom for the next few days after that. This was like that, but also strange as it became more intense, with an occasional stab. And unlike the other pain, where she could feel it isolated to one spot, this seemed to move around inside.

"This way," Madame Styvia said. Her hand pointed off the road to the right. Father Lucian followed her direction and led the line of individuals on to a crushed stone path. When Sarah stepped off the road, a sharp pain hit her like a bolt, and sent her to her knees. She didn't say anything, or groan, but somehow her three escorts knew and had stopped and turned to look at her. Fear dripped from their face.

Sarah got up and took another step. Again, another sharp pain, followed by a tightening and twisting of her stomach. Someone or something was trying to tie it into knots, and from the feeling of it, they had succeeded and were going for a double knot. This didn't send her to the ground, but it wasn't for lack of trying. Sarah toughed through it to try to assure the others she was okay. By the third hit, Father Lucian and Madame Styvia had taken notice.

"I am fine," croaked Sarah. "Just my stomach."

"Are you sure that is it?", Madame Styvia asked with the concern of the iceberg that hit the Titanic.

There was no way Sarah would admit how bad the pain was. Showing any signs of weakness would just give her one more reason not to trust her. Even when

Sister Genevieve reached back for her, Sarah brushed her away, and gutted out three steps to reach the others and a sight that momentarily distracted her from the pain. No one had explained to her what she might see at the Hill of a Thousand Crosses. The image her mind constructed was a large grass cover hill with white crosses running up and down it. Like the memorial in Normandy she had visited once with Father Lucian, on a rather simple matter. What she wouldn't give for something as simple as just sending an old honorable vet to a place he can finally find eternal peace now.

What she saw were crosses of all types, shapes, and sizes lining the path that led them up to an elongated rise in the ground, where there were more crosses. It was astonishing and horrifying to see. Instead of seeing the crosses in the ground, they were floating above the ground, in what Sarah had to assume was not their natural state. The ones closest to them shook as they passed.

"Father, how close do you think we need to be to fix the seal?", Sarah asked. Her voice trembled, as did her hands. Any concern about seeming weak had disappeared. Erased by the fear that had moved in.

"We must be on top of the hill," he said, sounding as stone solid as always.

They continued forward. Sarah forced each step, even though the pain had increased to the point where she had started to pant. The number of crosses around them increased the closer they came to the hill itself. All floating. All shook as they passed. Now they rattled against one another, creating an ear shattering sound that Sarah knew was a warning, like the tail of a rattlesnake. The warning had been heard, but not heeded. A slender set of concrete stairs came into view ahead of them. It led up the hill itself through the sea of floating and rattling wood, stone, and metal crosses. They were no more than ten feet away when it all happened. A pain unlike anything Sarah had felt before sent her to the ground. It was a good thing, too. Several crosses flew at her, slashing through the area she had been standing. If she hadn't fallen, they would have impaled her. Her three escorts dropped next to her to avoid another volley.

Amid the horrifying rattle and crashes of wood, stone, and metal smashing into the surrounding ground, she heard Madame Styvia yelling commands at the crosses as they came past her. She stood her ground and held out a familiar looking cross. A white light blasted forward from it, melting the projectiles on contact. Sarah saw Father Lucian beside the warrior, but something was wrong. He was knelt down on one knee, and his head hung down. Madame Styvia was protecting him. In fact, she was protecting all of them, or trying to. A few crosses still made it through behind her and crossed above Sarah and her escort's heads. After seeing one almost take out Madame Styvia from behind, Sarah forced herself up, but only made it as far as a single knee, with one hand still propped on the ground. The other hand held up behind them. In it, the cross of her own. Not of the sacred wood like the one Madame

Styvia had, just a simple gold cross, but it did what it needed to and focused Sarah's power and shot its own beam of truth out, brighter than that of Madame Styvia, blasting the approaching crosses and continuing on to destroy those floating in the surrounding distance.

The attack stopped, and both Madame Styvia and Sarah put away their crosses. Those that floated around them rose up and exploded down into the ground with a thunderous boom. Each now stood firm in place, upside down upon the holy ground.

Sarah saw Madame Styvia hunched over Father Lucian and crawled up to his side. Her teacher, her rock, her center, knelt there with a simple rusted iron cross through the right side of his chest just below the collar bone. Blood soaked his stole and black coat. The stone solid confidence was gone from his eyes. Mortality had set in, and Sarah could see in them the fear of his own end.

5

"Hang with us, Father!", exclaimed Sarah. She cradled his head in the back of the car as they sped down the barren road and back to the burning and half destroyed village. Madame Styvia and Sister Cecelia were in the front.

"Turn here!", directed Madame Styvia. The driver yanked the car to the left, slamming the occupants around. Father Lucian let out a groan. Sarah tried to keep him as still as possible, but there was only so much she could do.

"Two blocks and a right!"

Sarah attempted to brace herself and the Father for the next turn. She did better this time. Using her body as a cushion against the door. One hand cradled his head on her lap, the other hand pressed down on his stole, which was now balled up covering the gushing wound. When the car straightened on the road, Sarah looked up at the surrounding buildings. Large cracks plagued what stone covered front facades not already in piles of rubble on the ground. Every so often there was a building that was nothing more than a pile of rubble now. There were no fires on this road, but plenty of distraught survivors. All watched as they approached and continued to watch as the car passed by them. Sarah had to wonder how much these villagers know of what was really going on out there.

"The third house on the next block... on the right!", barked Madame Styvia.

"We are almost there, Father," Sarah said to Father Lucian. His eyes were closed, and his breathing labored.

The car slammed to a stop, and Madame Styvia exploded out and yanked open the back door. Sarah almost fell out backward, but caught herself. She stepped out, but leaned into the car to keep pressure on Father Lucian's wound.

"We need help!", Madame Styvia yelled toward the dark brown wooden door. It burst open as if her voice had ordered it to do so, and two men in dark suits and black hats rushed outside. One ran around the other side of the car and opened the backdoor on that side. The other came to Sarah's side and placed his hands under the Fathers' shoulders.

"Sister, we are going to lift him. You maintain pressure." the man said in a thick eastern European accent. Sarah backed away from the car while the man lifted and pulled Father Lucian from the backseat. The man on the other side came through the car holding the Father's legs. Once both were out, Sarah placed her blood stained hand back on the stole in an attempt to stop the flow of blood. It was a battle she was losing.

A second car pulled up behind with the other two sisters as Sarah squeezed in through the door with Father Lucian. The inside looked like the inside of any normal home, but the furniture in all three rooms she could see had been pushed to the side clearing the center of the room. Banks of candles and flashlights provided the only illumination. This was now a makeshift field hospital, with bodies lying on sheets on the floor as people ran from one person to the next, tending to them the best they could. Blood-soaked bandages dotted each patient, showing where their injuries were. Moans and screams identified the most severally injured.

"Doctor Johhan. Over here. The Father has been injured!", Madame Styvia screamed.

A man with white sleeves rolled up to his elbows, blood stained skin below that, stood up and rushed toward the group that was now just inside the door. His bearded face bore the stress and weariness of a man with more patients than he could handle. His eyes told Sarah it was not within his nature to try. After a quick look at Father Lucian, he gave a quick direction, "there", pointing to an empty spot in the front room.

Sarah followed the men as they laid Father Lucian down on the spot. Doctor Johhan knelt down and removed the stole, and ripped away Father Lucian's jacket and shirt. Blood pulsated from the gaping hole in Father Lucian's chest. The doctor sprung up and ran through the maze of patients to a table in the other room. There was a rattle of objects on the table, before he turned and rushed back to the Father's side. They positioned two clamps on either end of a severed artery, stopping the loss of blood.

"This is the best I can do. I am not equipped to repair the artery here. He needs a hospital," he said. His hands pinched the wound together and pressed a single suture through the skin from one side. Father Lucian moaned, and his body jerked. "I am sorry, Father. I am out of pain killer," he said, pulling it through and going in for a second pass. He made three complete passes through and then tied it off. "That will hold, but it is all I can do."

"Where is the closest hospital?", Sarah asked.

"It was twenty minutes away, but it was destroyed in the quake. As was the next closest one, Sister." Sarah saw the despair in his eyes. "William!", he called across the room. A boy no more than thirteen ran across to him. His eyes shell shocked. They exchanged words in a language Sarah didn't speak, and then the boy took off through the front door. "I have heard the Red Crescent and military were setting up one at the airport. My son will find out. "

Madame Styvia looked around the rooms. She found another boy, tall and slender. Sarah would guess he was probably sixteen or seventeen. After a few words, he took off out the front door as well. "Gordia will grab William and take the car. It won't take them long to find out."

Sarah and her escorts stayed knelt around Father Lucian, who was still unresponsive. They attempted to stay out of the way, but that was easier said than done in the crowded confines of the room. It wasn't long before she heard cries of, "Sister. Sister!", from across the room. Sarah looked in the voice's direction, but didn't see who had said it. She heard it again, and this time saw an elderly man trying to prop himself up on his elbow as he looked in their direction.

"These are people of strong faith. They want a prayer for their safety," Madame Styvia said to Sarah, her tone toxic and irritating to Sarah. "Can you spare one of them to maybe help these soldiers of Christ?" She pointed to the Sisters.

"Yes," Sarah responded and then told Sister Angelica to go tend to the man. Others began to cry out for them. A few were more seriously injured than the others. Sarah felt it pull at her on the inside. She had been tending to the sick and needy for many years now. "I can help as well."

"You?", shot back Madame Styvia. "You have taken the vows?"

"Yes," Sarah confidently replied, and she showed her the silver ring on her left hand signaling her commitment to the church.

"Blasphemy," spat Madame Styvia. "You are anything but worthy."

"I think you underestimate me and who I am," shot back Sarah. She didn't wait to ask for permission, and summoned Sister Genevieve to come with her as she made her way to the closest person requesting assistance. A woman, not much older than Sarah, laid there with a gash across her forehead and cuts up and down her arms. A homemade splint on her left leg. Hope filled her eyes as she looked up at Sarah.

"Pray with me, Sister," she pleaded in a weak voice.

"Of course, what is your name?", Sarah asked as she placed her hand on the only uninjured area she saw, her shoulder.

"Lillian," she said.

Sarah bowed her head and prayed, "Almighty and Eternal God. You are the everlasting health of those who believe in you. Hear us for Your sick servant Lillian, for who we implore the aid of Your tender mercy, that being restored to physical health, she may give thanks to You. Through Christ, our Lord. Amen."

"Thank you, Sister," the woman said.

"Now rest. Let your faith heal you," Sarah said as she stood up and searched for where to go to next. Doctor Johhan approached her and pointed out a man in the next room, and explained he was close to death. Before he even asked, Sarah knew what the request was. She hadn't given Last Rites before, but knew how, and proceeded to the man.

He was semiconscious while Sarah gave him his Last Rites, and out of compassion, she repeated sections of it to allow him to respond instead of moving on. There was a fear in his eyes, but as she finished, she heard his breathing slow and a look of peace filled his eyes. It stayed there even after his last breath escaped his lungs. She sat peacefully over him for a moment, reflecting before moving to the next. That peace was shattered, as the voice of a man from across the home screamed, "You!" Sarah turned to see a blinding light come at her, and then knock her against the wall of the room, several feet away.

6

"What the hell?", Sarah exclaimed. Sister Genevieve rushed to her side, but Sarah motioned her away while she dusted herself off. The hit from whatever it was hurt like nothing she had felt before, but there was something strangely familiar about it. Every head in the room, including those Sarah believed to be unconscious were now looking at one of two people. Her and the man stomping in her direction dressed like a modern day Dracula, putting away a familiar looking cross.

"Why you?," he spewed, marching toward Sarah through the maze of people. He never looked down, but maneuvered through it without a problem. "Don't we have enough to deal with... with that out there? Now you?"

"Marcus!", Styvia screamed, grabbing him just as his hand reached for Sarah's throat. It was inches short as Madame Styvia held him back. He continued to lunge trying to reach Sarah. His fingers stretching and squeezing, until Styvia pushed him back several feet and firmly placed herself between Sarah and the enraged man. A hand still on the vest covered chest of the man. "Father Lucian brought her."

This news didn't seem to settle the man down. He pulled back from Madame Styvia's touch and paced back and forth, leering around at Sarah and mumbling the whole time.

Madame Styvia grabbed him by the shoulders. "I'm not thrilled about it either, but we have bigger problems." She then turned to Sarah, "Don't take this as an approval for you being here. It's not, and for the rest of the time you are here, you are to not go near the hill. Understood?" Before Sarah could answer, she answered for her. "Good."

"Not good enough. I want her out of here. Now!... And... and," he stammered. "That outfit she has on. That is a crime against God."

"What is your problem?", Sarah asked, rather pissed off herself. She felt her temper starting up. This time it was all her.

"See, she doesn't even sound like a nun." The man scoffed at her and then dismissed her with his right hand.

"Sarah Meyer. Meet Lord Marcus Negiev. The keeper responsible for this site, and one that met you in Miller's Crossing."

Not again.

"Hi," she said, sounding unsure of herself, and still pissed. With how he reacted to her, she had no doubt something horrible happened. Of course, Sarah didn't know what happened, and Father Lucian refused to tell her ever. He always told her to focus on the future and leave the past behind. Which she found ironic, so much of her life was learning about the past to prepare for the future.

"I assume that thing is still with you," barked Lord Negiev.

"Yes. Always.", replied Sarah.

"Bah. This is stupid," he protested. "I don't care who brought her here. Where is he? We need to talk." The pale man in a black suit and grey vest scanned the room violently.

"Over there." Madame Styvia pointed to Father Lucian lying on the floor with blood soaked bandages covering him.

"Oh my. What happened to him?" Lord Negiev rushed to Father Lucian's side.

"We went to the hill, and it threw crosses at us. He was hit, and severely wounded," Madame Styvia said, pained. "We are trying to find a medical facility we can rush him to. Gordia and William have gone to see if there is a field hospital at the airport. They should be back soon."

"Father. Father. Father. You are going to be okay," Lord Negiev knelt by the unconscious priest and stroked his head. Other than the slow rise and drop of Father Lucian's chest with each breath, he looked lifeless. "This is because of her isn't it?" The care that was in his voice moments ago had drained away, allowing his venom to fill in behind it.

His repeated comments and accusations had created an air of anger in the room, and Sarah was its target. The curious eyes that had looked at her earlier now echoed his rage, darkening the already desperation filled room. She was cornered and didn't like it. Her younger self would have lashed back, but her more mature self just stood there and absorbed it all.

"Stop it!," Madame Styvia shot back at Lord Negiev. "She was there yes, but it was not because of her. It attacked us all. If you want to blame anyone, blame me. I was next to him and missed one."

He let it drop, which didn't surprise Sarah. She knew if she had been the one who missed she would be flying up against the wall again.

"Let's just help who we can while we wait on William and Gordia," Madame Styvia said. "Then, you and I have something to take care of."

"And she will stay here!", Lord Negiev added forcefully.

Sarah waited to see if the other keeper would object, but she didn't and instead moved to help the doctor the best she could. Lord Negiev stayed next to Father Lucian. He spoke to him softly while stroking his forehead with occasional looks at his wound to check the bleeding. Sarah noticed a few of the occasional looks at the wound ended with a glare in her direction.

While the others were doing that, Sarah and Genevieve returned to what they were doing before she was thrown against a wall and sat and prayed with the hurt and suffering. The first few she tended to were hesitant to participate. A remnant of the air of hatred that hung in the room, but after Sarah started that appeared to melt away each time.

The tension that built inside her disappeared as she tended to her duties. It gave her a serenity she had never felt in her life before the convent. To this day, she still remembered the first time she sat with an ill woman and prayed with her in her home in the village of Fiesole. The woman was so caring and accepting, as most Sarah tended to were. And, she wasn't the first Sarah had tended to. Each gave her a feeling of peace, but this one time Sarah could sense the peace and tranquility she gave her. She only paused from her duties when the door opened, as most did to see if there was a new patient to rush and tend to immediately. Sarah wanted to see if the two boys had returned yet with news of the field hospital.

Sarah was growing tired, and concerned, as it had been a while, and many prayers, since the boys left. She had made her way all the way from the front room to two rooms back. From there she could barely hear the opening of the door over the moans and wails. She heard what sounded like the door again, but by the time she looked, it was still closed. She returned to give the man she was tending to, hope; a hope she felt leaving her as the time passed. She wanted to stop what she was doing and go to Father Lucian's side, but not with Lord Negiev there. Nothing could get her that close to that man, and Sarah was pretty sure he wanted it that way too.

7

"It is there!" William and Gordia exploded through the door and ran to Doctor Johhan.

"Hold up, William," Gordia cried, out of breath and bent over just inside the door. "It was there. The road is destroyed. Looks like an aftershock took out the airport," he gasped," and everything in it. You can see the tents they set up... all over the ground... mostly on fire."

Doctor Johhan tossed William's hair. "Thanks for trying, William. You too Gordia." He turned to walk back to his patients. To Sarah, he looked to be a man defeated and drained of all hope. He needed that field hospital to be there. Not just for Father Lucian, but for most of the people in the building. This place was nothing more than a place to triage and stabilize, if possible. It wasn't equipped for anything more. The more Sarah thought about it, the more she could relate to how the doctor felt. This was now a place of death, and there was nothing anyone could do to stop it.

Sarah's gaze moved to Father Lucian, and her heart sank the rest of the way into the pit of despair that surrounded her. A tear trickled down her cheek. A second one followed. When the third one attempted to join them, she sniffed and rubbed it away. She needed to be strong. Not for herself. Not for Father Lucian, he wouldn't know the difference in his current state. Not for the other keepers, Sarah didn't really care what they thought of her. It was everyone else. Everyone else that was going to die here and would need comforting. Father Lucian would expect her to do her duty and provide that, and that was what she was going to do.

There was one more gaze in Father Lucian's direction before Sarah went on about her duty. Some final words, and another tear. Madame Styvia and Lord Negiev were doing the same. Both leaned over the Father's body. Sarah knelt down over a woman who, like the Father, was unconscious. Doctor Johhan told her she wouldn't wake up again and wouldn't last the hour. Sarah started a prayer to comfort her soul when, out of the corner of her eye, she saw Madame Styvia and Lord Negiev heading for the door. Sarah stood, still praying.

Everyone not injured or tending to the injured ran to them. They shook their hands, and exchanged hugs and words of luck. Sarah didn't need to be told where they were going and why. The looks both of them gave her told her she wasn't going with them. No matter how much she tried. And just to make sure it was clear, Lord Negiev yelled, "You stay here!". They were out the door.

Sarah thought about running after them, and she wasn't the only one. Sister Genevieve had already started for the door when Sarah stood up. She looked back at Father Lucian laying there, his breathing shallow and labored. He brought her there to do what they were going to do, but they were keepers as well. They were just as capable as she was. The sounds around the rooms reminded her that, she could do something they couldn't, and she knelt back down.

Over the next half hour, they lost more than half of those they attempted to save. Between Sarah and the other sisters, they managed to give each a peaceful passing, which was the best they could do. Sarah wished there was more. During that time, the ground under them rumbled several times. A few small aftershocks, and one large one that brought down large chunks of plaster from the ceiling, adding to the persistent dust cloud that was everywhere you looked. Even from where Sarah was, she could tell the job hadn't been completed. It was still out there.

Doctor Johhan collapsed to the wall and slid to the floor next to Sarah. He was exhausted, and at the moment had no one left that needed treatment. The only victims left had minor cuts and bruises, and a few broken bones, but they were all stable. No one new had come in for hours. Which was also another sad benchmark. It meant there was no one else out there.

Sarah handed him a handkerchief she used to wipe blood and dirt off her hands as she went from person to person. He turned it to a clean side and wiped his forehead. She saw trails through the dust that lined his face telling of the tears he had shed. As his face relaxed, the areas of clean skin in the folds of his brow and the corners of his mouth told of how long his expression had been clinched. His eyes stared at the floor lined with bodies, more covered from head to toe by blankets than not. He had won a few battles today, but Sarah could tell from the tremble in his chin it wasn't enough.

"So why do they hate you?", he asked in a whisper.

That was the question, and Sarah didn't have a good answer, so she gave him the only answer she knew that wouldn't create any additional questions. "We met once before, and it didn't go well."

"It's more than that. I haven't seen Marcus do what he did to you to another person before."

"So, you know what he is?", Sarah asked, unprepared for that.

"A keeper?," he asked. "Yes, most of us do. It's no great secret around here, but we are great at keeping secrets." He pointed in the direction of the hill.

"I guess that's true," Sarah said. Sarah remembered how others in Miller's Crossing knew the truth about their family, even when they didn't. They guarded the secret, much like here. It was probably the same for everyone. A circle of trustees.

"Are you a keeper?"

"Me, no," Sarah said, and then added, "My father and brother are."

"It runs in families, doesn't it?", he asked, sounding more curious than exhausted. Sarah nodded. "Then that makes you a keeper as well. So why did another keeper attack you?"

If the question didn't tell Sarah that Doctor Johhan wasn't letting this go, the fact that he had turned to face her made it loud and clear. She needed a good answer that would satisfy his curiosity. Of course, the moment she needed creativity, the stress, death, and exhaustion she had experienced stifled her ability to come up with anything even believable. Even the truth seemed too out there for most to believe, but knowing he could keep a secret she tried that. "There is a little more to me than you can see. A demon possessed and hasn't let go. It's kept dormant by the prayers performed by the sisters who travel with me."

"A demon?", was his only response.

"Yea, a demon," Sarah said, and noticed a concern and almost fear in his eyes. "Don't worry. It's under control."

"Good," his voice said, still sounding unsure. "Is it safe to assume they had something to do with you and the demon?"

Sarah pressed her face into her hands. She rubbed her eyes, and then massaged her temples before she answered, with her hands still muffling her voice, "They battled the demon to rescue me, or so I have figured out."

"You don't remember?"

"No," Sarah said. "I wish I did, but I don't remember anything but a few slivers here and there. And, those were like watching the most horrifying movie. I have asked, but they won't tell."

"Huh," Doctor Johhan said, and then paused, seemingly lost in thought before he continued. "Good clinical practice there. You don't want to fill in too many details for someone that suffered a severe traumatic event. It could do irreparable psychological harm."

"So, I have been told," Sarah said, wondering if knowing you carried a demon could do similar harm.

"And now? Do you follow Father Lucian around to help as some sort of repentance?", he looked upon Sarah with inquisitive and trusting eyes. She saw no signs of a man afraid of sitting next to a woman possessed by a powerful demon. Why would he? They live with one under their very feet every day. It was refreshing. Sarah always dreaded the day someone found out what she was. The world would fear her as the devil itself. Not here.

"Yes and no. It enhances my abilities and..." a commotion coming through the door interrupted Sarah's explanation, causing both of them to spring to their feet. A cloud of dust rushed in through the door, along with Madame Styvia helping Lord Negiev in. It was obvious to Sarah, their attempt hadn't gone well. The ground growled beneath her feet.

8

"What happened?", Sarah asked alarmed.

Madame Styvia helped Lord Negiev down to the floor. He had been roughed up from head to toe. Bruises and cuts covered his body. The neat black suit he left in, was nothing more than tattered cloth now. He landed on the ground with a moan, but was alive and responsive. His hand reached out for Styvia, which she didn't see, and it landed on her leg, but did not grab. It patted her, as if to thank her for dragging him back. "Marcus made a suggestion, that IT did not like," Madame Styvia said, out of breath.

"Ala?", asked Sarah.

What life that was left in Lord Negiev propelled him up to his feet, and he stumbled toward her. Everyone else looked at her stunned. Madame Styvia once again found herself playing peacekeeper, placing herself between Sarah and Marcus. She caught him in her arms and said, "She doesn't know," rather calmly, and helped Marcus back to the ground with the assistance of Doctor Johhan who had already began to examine the torn bits of flesh on Marcus's arms.

"Sister," Madame Styvia turned to Sarah and said, "We don't use the name. Using the name is akin to inviting the demon in."

Just then Sarah remembered her lessons, and the importance of a demon's name. Knowing and speaking a demon's name basically opens a direct line of communication with the creature. It can either invite them in, or cast them out. That is why there is such focus on identifying the demon before taking any action. It helps to know what you are dealing with, and it gives you the true upper hand. "I forgot my lesson. I am sorry."

"It's okay," she said. The tension that existed in her tone earlier was gone. Was it a case she was warming up to Sarah, or worn down by exhaustion? Sarah didn't know. Either way she would take it. "The seal is more than cracked. The ground is showing cracks radiating out from the hill. It won't be long until it finds a weak spot and gets out."

"Father Lucian said," Sarah caught herself about to say the name again, "IT ... was responsible for bad weather. What else can you tell me?"

"Bad weather. If it was only that. It manipulates the forces of nature, so yes, weather, but also fire, ice, floods, you name the natural disaster, and it can summon it. In 1813, it rained over three villages north of here for three solid months, flooding farmlands, drowning livestock, and destroying stored crops. In 1837, there was an eruption sending balls of fire hundreds of miles in all directions. The ensuing wildfires burnt villages to the ground before those living there could get out. In 1848, a flood appeared out of nowhere wiping two villages off the map. None of the hundreds of people that lived in them were ever found. Mind you, there are no rivers in this area that could supply that amount of water, and we are still hundreds of miles from the Baltic Sea. Then in 1850, we were hit by a blizzard, which isn't that out of the ordinary considering where we are, but not in August. The ground stayed frozen until the next spring, killing crops and..."

"I get the picture," interrupted Sarah, "But why? What does it have to gain by destroying farms and villages? Don't demons want something?"

"They do, just not always for themselves," Madame Styvia said. She walked to Sarah, joining her against the wall Sarah sat against having a leisure conversation with Doctor Johhan in the moments before their return. "Remember this is all part of a bigger war. The war of good and evil. The war of God and all else."

"Destruction of faith," they both said together.

"Yes, imagine you are a God-fearing individual. You go to church. You pray and worship. You give of yourself, and what do you receive in return? Destruction. No protection from the very evil the bible says He will protect the penitent from. What I told you were just the large events in the history of this region, but before IT was locked away, there were little things. Single farms, or a couple here and there. Massacres of livestock. Those litter the tales the old timers would tell you. Marcus could tell you a few others. Now I will say after a while everything that goes bad becomes IT's fault. We don't know which of those minor events were truly IT's doing or not, but that should tell you the kind of oppression the people felt with it around."

"Oppression? The cover story? The pope's plaque?", Sarah wondered aloud.

"Makes sense now, doesn't it?"

It sure did. Father Lucian told Sarah the hill of crosses was a monument to the strength of the Lithuanian people and all the oppression they had suffered under the Russians and Germans during the World Wars. It was a monument to the strength and the oppression, and the World Wars gave a good cover story the public would believe, it now all made sense. The constant rumbling of the ground signaled that oppression wanted to return.

"What now?", Sarah asked.

"Well," started Madame Styvia. "We have to go back out there and try to finish this. If you are willing?"

She looked at Sarah with kind eyes, but Sarah remembered her initial reaction and was surprised by the question. "Are you sure you trust me? You didn't seem too happy about seeing me here, and told me I wasn't to go anywhere near the hill."

"Well, you have to remember what Marcus and I went through the first time we met," Sarah started to interrupt, and her hands flew up wildly with her irritation, but Madame Styvia grabbed them, gently. "I know. That was not you, that was him, and I am sure you don't remember anything. Most never do. It was one of the most challenging times as Keepers, and even then, we didn't win. You are more of a stalemate." That term turned the screw a little more inside Sarah. Words were pressing against her lips to get out. "But, Father Lucian trusts you, and he has told us about the work you and he have done. Is it true, your friend's presence enhances your abilities?"

This woman had a way with words, and not in a good way, but Sarah understood the message and the question. Sarah bit her lip. "I wouldn't call him my friend, more of a passenger, and yes, from what I can tell his presence does. I don't need a relic to focus my abilities."

"In that I am jealous, Sister"

"What about him?", Sarah asked looking over at Lord Negiev.

"I wouldn't worry about him. He is in no shape to go back out there, or to stop you and I from going. IT threw tons of pieces of dirt at him, in an attempt to bury him. The sticks and twigs that were in the wave of earth made it through and cut him up pretty good. I think a stone got him in the head too, but he will be okay. I am worried about the Father. We can't get him help until we end this." She looked in the direction of the unconscious Father Lucian. "If we seal IT back up, maybe the quakes will stop and we will have a chance," Madame Styvia said, with a glint in her eye that told Sarah she truly believed that. "Just focus on that, and we can help him."

Sarah looked back at Father Lucian again and watched him. His breathing had become more labored and erratic. Sister Cecelia was still knelt by him and tending to him. She looked up and shook her head, with a grave look on her face. He didn't have long, and Sarah knew it. Something inside her felt him slipping away.

"Shall we?", Madame Styvia asked as if she were asking Sarah to go shopping. She stood up and dusted off her long black dress. Dust and debris had gathered in the ruffles and covered the accents of dark red from her view. A quick shake of her head sent the dust flying from her long raven hair. She headed for the door. Sarah followed with Sister Genevieve.

"No, you can't," cried Lord Negiev as they walked past him. He sat up, reaching toward them.

"Not her. You can't..." he cried again, but those were the last words he screamed before his mind succumbed to the pain rendering him unconscious.

9

The clock on the tower in the classic tree-lined walkway and bench littered town square said it was mid-afternoon, but it looked more like late evening. Clouds of smoke and dust still billowed up around them, blocking out the sun, and casting the entire town into a hazy dusk appearance. The landscape was nothing but browns and greys everywhere, like an aged picture. Denser clouds rose from just beyond the horizon, giving it an ominous appearance, like the shadow of a great beast lurking in the haze. If only it wasn't true, but in part it was. And that is why the three women walked toward it.

The use of a car was now out of the question. It appeared in the hours Sarah was inside, other buildings had fallen. Their stone facades were now nothing more than piles of rubble that stretched out into the street. Difficult as it was to climb, they would have been impossible to drive over. Some of the rumbles she had felt were probably the buildings making their last statement in this world before becoming just piles of stone and dust.

"So, that prayer, it's like a seal?", Madame Styvia asked, breaking the silence that had existed between them. Not that Sarah minded the silence. The quiet gave her a moment to think about what was ahead of them, and what to do about it. Her experience to date had been limited to lost spirits and what in the grand scheme of the world were lesser demons. Not that her lessons at the Vatican didn't cover this. But reading stories and recounts of events that happened centuries ago didn't replace practical experience.

"Yea, I guess it is," Sarah agreed. She hadn't thought about it that way before, but it was a type of seal. One placed on her by the other sisters. One that required constant maintenance, care, and feeding by the prayer. "The prayer keeps it in place and maintains its strength. Was there something similar on the hill?", asked Sarah, but then she answered her own question. "The crosses?"

"Yes, the crosses," Madame Sylvia said. "Every week a pilgrimage is made to the hill. They anoint the cross with oil and then dip the bottom spike in holy water before plunging into the ground."

Sarah thought about that for a moment. *Could it be that simple?* It was hard to believe. There may be no need for a battle with this beast, just another cross to lock it back in. With a ton of hope, she asked, "Then we just need to do that again to lock it back."

"Yes, that is true," Madame Styvia answered, straining as she crawled up an enormous pile of debris that blocked the road out of town. It was a combination of mangled buildings, cars, trees, and chunks of ground.

Sarah thought back to her own experiences again. She had discounted them before, but may have been quick to do so. Each was formidable in their own right. But what made them a challenge was not the challenge here. She knew exactly what needed to happen. There was no great mystery to unravel, secret to find, or truth to uncover. This was just a simple, go take that hill, and plunge a cross into the heart of the hill.

From the top of the mound, Madame Styvia stood tall and looked down at Sarah and Sister Genevieve as they climbed up. "Of course, the challenge is even getting close enough to be able to do that." A fact that the true gravity of didn't hit Sarah until she joined Styvia at the top of the mound and looked out at the landscape ahead of them.

Every time Sarah thought she had seen hell on Earth, hell upped its game, but none of them held a candle to this sight. The fire and brimstone of Hades' front porch would have been a vacation spot compared to this. The ground wasn't cracked, it was shattered. Flames roared up through the ruptures as if they were the exhales of the beast underneath. Smoke hovered just above the ground to capture the glow of the flames underneath and letting no light from above through. It smelled of a noxious sulfur. Sarah gasped at the sight.

"Bad, huh?", Madame Styvia asked as she stepped down the pile of rubble.

"I have never seen anything so...", Sarah started, but couldn't find the right word that matched what her eyes saw.

"I did once, it was worse."

Sarah followed her down the pile. Being careful with every step not to land on a loose piece that would slip underneath her. It wasn't the easiest of tasks, but she managed, and every few steps she turned around to make sure Sister Genevieve was doing okay. The sister appeared to be following Sarah's exact steps down the pile. Her attention was down at the rubble, but she kept up her duty.

"It was when we came for you," Madame Styvia said.

She was at the bottom waiting on them, looking straight up at Sarah when she said it. Her look didn't tell Sarah if she was just making an observation or if there was something more behind it. It was business like, as was her tone. Which Sarah understood. Knowing where they were heading had forced her focus on the task at hand. She hadn't even thought about Father Lucian since they left, but she felt there was something there she needed to clear out of the air. "Look, I am not sure what happened back then. No one had told me. I am sorry for whatever it was."

"I know. It's just, this reminds me of that moment," Madame Styvia said. "But then there were more of us. Are you sure of your abilities?"

Sarah proceeded down the pile and once at the bottom she said, "Yes, very." She wasn't, not compared to what they had to deal with, but there wasn't a chance in hell she was going to admit that. Madame Styvia had finally stopped looking at her with contempt, Sarah wasn't about to give her a reason to start again.

"Are you sure that thing is under control?"

"That I am sure of. It hasn't been out since you last saw me," Sarah answered. This answer was the complete truth, and she looked Madame Styvia right in the eyes as she delivered it.

"Just needed to be sure. Let's go."

Sarah helped Sister Genevieve down off the pile, and the three women walked across the broken landscape into the mouth of hell itself. The smell was horrible and burned Sarah's nose, but the heat was the worst. It was oppressive, and Sarah was sweating up a storm in her habit, so much so she removed her headpiece and balled it up in her hand, but not before rolling up the sleeves of her tunic. Her comment to Sister Genevieve, "Not a word to Mother," drew a half-hearted laugh from Madame Styvia. Though it wasn't more than a few moments before she rolled up her sleeves as well.

Sister Genevieve kept her prayer up and showed no distress from the crucible they traveled through, but Sarah knew she was hot and miserable as well, and also knew her well enough to know she wouldn't discard any portions of her habit for comfort. Her faith, duty, and position were above her own comfort, and Sarah knew not to push that too far. But that didn't stop Sarah from reaching over and pushing up the sleeves of her wool garment. It was something Sarah knew the sister wouldn't have done on her own.

They worked through the maze of explosions of flame and smoke. Small patches of earth blasted skyward with each. A few particles of dirt rained down on them as they walked, or tried to. The ground had a constant rumble that grew more intense the closer they came to the hill. Like a wild animal's warning that became louder the closer you got to it. Sarah knew it was only a matter of time before this animal snapped at them and tried to bite. The bark was terrifying, and she had a feeling this was not one of those occasions when the bark was worse than the bite.

10

When the Hill came into view, it didn't resemble the place Sarah had seen that morning. It didn't resemble a hill at all. It was a piece of earth that rose and fell with every breath of the great beast. A dark blood red hue bathed the world around them, and waves of heat radiated up from the ground.

As they got closer, the rumble, the growl of the beast, turned into a laugh. Sarah noticed Madame Styvia had removed the cross from around her neck and held it firmly in her hand in front of her. Sarah did the same and spoke a quick blessing. "Lord, watch over us as we spread your righteousness to this foul beast. Give us the strength to overcome the evil with in. Give us the guidance to do what is needed to protect all of your servants from it. In God's name. Amen." There was a quick flash from both of the crosses and Madame Styvia looked at Sarah surprised, but said nothing.

They pushed on to the edge of the crosses. Again, this was a place Sarah believed she stood earlier, but nothing looked familiar. Gone was the worn path created by the hundreds upon thousands of pilgrims that visited the site every year. Also gone were the stairs that lead you up the slight rise to the top of the hill. All that remained were the thousands of crosses stuck upside down in the massive heaving spot of ground.

Sarah heard the deep rumbling laugh again, and said, "We amuse it."

"Yep, but I am not amused." Madame Styvia marched off the path and grabbed the first cross she came to and yanked it up. The ground heaved and screamed, and fought to keep its hold of the object. She pulled back with all her might and the ground lost the battle, giving up the object and sent her falling to the ground with a thud, but with the iron cross in her hand. "Cover me," she yelled, as the ground jerked and shook violently.

Sarah managed to keep her feet, but Sister Genevieve fell to the ground. Sarah positioned herself over her fellow sister and kept her head on a swivel, looking from anything and everything. "What is going to happen?", she exclaimed.

"This is when the storm of dirt hit Marcus before. I just need a few minutes."

During one of the quick spins of her head, Sarah saw Madame Styvia pull out a vial from a pocket. She knew immediately what she was doing and directed Sister Genevieve to slide closer to the other keeper so she could cover them both. She paused her protective scan long enough to watch Madame Styvia expertly anoint the cross in oil and then drip three drops of holy water on the bottom of the ornamental iron cross. One drop ran down it and dripped on the ground. A column of steam exploded upward from the ground, knocking all three women backward. Sarah felt the great rush of steam on her face, but was merely made uncomfortable, not burned. The same for Sister Genevieve. Madame Styvia wasn't so lucky. The scalding jet caught both hands, and her left cheek. She fell to the ground, and appeared to scream, her injured hands held out, but Sarah couldn't hear the scream. The howling that came from all around them drowned out the injured woman's painful wails.

Sister Genevieve moved to help Madame Styvia, and Sarah stood guard over the top of both of them. She expected anything, crosses, sticks, or rocks to come flying at them, and didn't wait to start reciting the various prayers that had served her well through the years. Some were prayers for the sick and dying. Others for traditional prayers to praise her Lord and Savior, but others were of a more personal nature. Ones that she had written and brought with her. Maybe that is why those were the ones she felt a deeper personal connection with. Around them the ground started to glow a bright white, not the dark blood red it had been, and it was quiet. There was no rumble. She could see the waves of the rumble in the surrounding ground approach, but stop at the edge for the ring of light. She continued to pray, and the ring expanded.

"I claim this space in your name," she said, concluding one of her personal prayers, and was about to start another one when she spotted something in the distance approaching them. It was the shadow of a creature that moved on all fours, like an animal. She blinked a few times to clear her vision of the tears caused by the heat and the putrid smell; hoping to see a deer or lost bear that hadn't run off when the earthquake hit. It wasn't an animal, or not at least one she recognized. The proportions of its shape were all wrong. The back legs were twice as long as the front, and had a short but slender frame. The back legs remained stiff with each step. Only the front appeared to bend. With the heat around, Sarah considered the possibility that it was an optical illusion. Like a mirage of water on the road on a hot and sunny day. The appearance of five more of those creatures dismissed that theory.

"Are you able to finish it?", Sarah asked with her voice shaking.
"I will try," Madame Styvia painfully responded.
"Okay, you might want to hurry."
"My hands are," Madame Styvia started. "What are those?"

It was clear to Sarah that she had seen what was now approaching them. "I don't know. Hurry. Please." Sarah took a sideways step to place herself firmly between the shadows and Styvia and Sister Genevieve. The first one was coming close enough to show itself. Now she could see why she thought it was a shadow. Its skin, if the leathery and scaled covered tissue she saw could be called skin, was the blackest black she had ever seen. So black, the light created by the flames didn't reflect off of them. They were just voids in the world. Two yellow eyes were on top of what she had to assume was its head. Short front legs resembled arms, but they didn't use them as such. They were short with a knee or elbow halfway up its length. Its movements appeared to consist of the front appendage reaching forward and clawing a hold in the ground, then its two long stick legs stumbled behind it. Not graceful, but she saw the potential for speed as one of them leapt forward and joined the others, covering a great distance in a single move.

Sarah started reciting her prayers again. And again, a ring of light surrounded them. Sarah's eyes closed, and she concentrated. Her hand reached up and gripped her cross. Feeling the shape of it was something that brought her comfort. Something she first experienced in feeling the worn wood of the relic entrusted to her family. This one was different. Simple and gold, but it worked the same. At first she thought it was just psychological, and then she considered the power of her faith. By accident she found something else though. She didn't need it to focus her abilities to sense or deal with spirits, but occasionally it did give her a boost, and it did again, sending the ring of light out from them a great distance. It seemed to clear the surrounding air this time, too. The putrid odor was gone, as was the smoke and heat. It was pleasant and a little chilly.

The creatures approached the edge of the ring. Sarah watched them intently as they stopped just short of the illuminated ground. She had seen this before and knew they wouldn't step foot inside. If they did, it would kill them. That was what had happened every time in the past. That was why seeing one finally step in, and not screech in pain or dissipate, sent Sarah gasping in fear.

After the first, the second followed, then the third, and finally all of them were again walking toward them, and getting closer, too close. The creatures didn't scream. They didn't howl. From Sarah's vantage point, she wasn't sure they had mouths. All she was sure of, they had sharp claws which were evident with each step.

"How much longer?", Sarah hastily asked.

"Not much."

Sarah looked back behind her at Madame Styvia who had cleaned off the large metal cross and once again was anointing it. Each movement told of the pain she felt in her hands as the oil stung her burns. Next was the holy water, and again Madame Styvia opened the vial and dropped three drops on the cross. This time she used the long skirt of her dress to cradle the cross to keep any drops from rolling off to the ground.

Sarah turned back around and found herself looking eye to eye with two yellow orbs in a sea of nothingness. The creature, not more than a foot away from her, appeared to study her, and still didn't make a sound. Sarah shrieked, making enough noise for everyone. The other creatures had fanned out and surrounded the three of them, but each had their attention on Sarah. Who had sucked the last of her shriek back in and was frantically rubbing at her cross, looking for just a bit of that comfort that it had provided her in the past.

Behind her, Madame Styvia had started a Latin prayer. Sarah heard her voice, but her attention was too focused on their visitors to hear the words. She watched its yellow eyes move from her to Madame Styvia who now held the cross up high above her head. In a single and violent move the creature slapped Sarah aside with its front legs, sending her crashing into another of the creatures which kicked her away with its metal rod like back leg. The pain was excruciating, but the image of all six creatures closing in on Madame Styvia with the cross up in the air, and Sister Genevieve, eyes closed and praying, gave her what she needed to spring up. In that single move, Sarah yanked her cross off her neck and made contact with the closest of the creatures. It shivered and shook and then disappeared. The ground rumbled as it did; the other creatures turned to her. For two of them, they turned too late. Sarah had already dismissed them. Another took a swipe at her from behind, and she ducked and slid under it, using the cross to slash at its otherworldly black skin. The creature fell flat on the ground before it disappeared.

This left two, which watched Sarah intently. They were now the prey, and they knew it. One backed away and moved for Madame Styvia, kicking her in the head with its back leg. The cross Madame Styvia had prepared flew up in the air. Sarah saw it and knew she had to finish this. She went to catch it, slashing a creature on the way. She didn't turn to watch its demise, her focus was the cross. It was also the focus of the remaining creature. The beast knew what it was and was there to stop it. Growing up in a household obsessed with baseball meant that at some point she would be shagging flies for her father or brother. Not because she was asked, but it was just something the whole family did together. Her father would pitch, Jacob would bat, and she was retrieving the balls. She knew to plan for the object she was chasing to drift a little further than it looked and overran where she thought it would land. Her left foot planted hard on the ground to stop her and gave her a powerful stance to lunge forward two steps to intercept the cross before the creature had its chance. She caught it, mid leap, and quickly oriented it with the spike down. As she came down, the creature was under her, making attempts to knock it from her grasp. Sarah held on firmly as she planted it deep in the ground and threw the slender body of the creature.

It disappeared, but Hell appeared. The ground under them swelled up like a balloon. Waves of heat blasted past them. Then on top of the hill, the ground broke, and fire blasted skyward thousands of feet. Sarah rushed to Sister Genevieve who was now helping the unconscious Madame Styvia. Sarah had finished what she had started, but this didn't look like a victory. She helped Sister Genevieve gather her up, and the two women carried the unconscious woman out of danger and back to the small village. The whole way, Sarah wondered, "What do we do now?"

11

    The journey back was an adventure Sarah wanted to quickly forget. Not only were she and Sister Genevieve carrying the in-and-out-of-consciousness Madame Styvia, they were surrounded by a world intent on killing them. The ground heaved around them with every step. Waves of heat and fire rushed at them. What buildings were left standing above the ground crumbled as they approached, and the debris appeared to be thrown in their direction. All while a continuous roar echoed from behind them. Their only protection was from the aura that radiated out from Sarah. How strong it was, surprised her. It even held a few times when she stopped praying. Every time in the past it had disappeared as soon as the words stopped, whether they were spoken or just in her head. It was as if something deep inside her was helping this time.

    Doctor Johan grabbed Madame Styvia as soon as they collapsed in through the door. Both Sarah and Sister Genevieve fell to their knees. Sarah felt like the weight of the world was off of her shoulders when the doctor and two other men took Madame Styvia, though she wouldn't doubt part of the relief she felt was she could now drop her guard. The sheer adrenaline of the attack at the hill had worn off some time ago, leaving her drained. Sister Angelica came over and checked on both of them. Both women tried to brush her off, but her concern didn't let her give in. She took up the duty while helping Sister Genevieve up before guiding her to a corner and forcing her to sit and let others tend to the scratches that covered her arms and face. Sarah hadn't even noticed them on her until that moment. There was no doubt Sarah was scratched and cut up too. The constant flashes of heat they faced out there had every inch of exposed skin feeling raw, covering the pain from any particular gash.

    Sarah wanted to sit down herself and rest, and knew she would, just not here, and forced herself to get up and walk across the room where she finally sprawled out along the side of Father Lucian; every muscle hurt, and she needed to release all the tension in her legs. Sister Cecelia sat on her knees tending to the Father. The look on her face told Sarah everything she needed to know about his condition. Tears had formed in the steadfast nun, though she never let them roll down her cheeks. Always wiping them away before they had a chance. Her cherub face that was known to bring smiles from all who saw her, now waved the flag of defeat. There was no smile, no glow, and no confidence. Sarah thought for a moment he had already passed, but a quick check caught the sight of his chest rising and then falling. What was worrisome is the pace of each breath had slowed down to a pace Sarah didn't know could support life, and each exhale sounded raspy. Fluid, probably blood, was now pooling in his lungs. There had to be a way to get him to help.

Sarah attempted to stand to go talk to several of the men who were helping Doctor Johhan tend to all the patients. She wanted to know if there were any options, no matter how remote. A large rumble along the ground, stronger than the regular growl that had occurred all day long, knocked her back to the ground. The flashlights in the room flickered and then shut off completely, leaving only the light of a few candles to illuminate the space. A strange silence crept in with the darkness. The rumbles, or growls, were gone. Both had been a constant since the quake. No wind outside, or crackling of the fires in the distance. Just the uneasy feeling of nothing. That was when Sarah realized she didn't hear breathing. Hers, Sister Cecelia's who was just across from her, or Father Lucian's. She looked down and saw his chest rise and fall, but there was no raspy sound as the air traveled through fluid and mucus in his lungs. Just behind Sister Cecelia, a woman adjusted a blanket that laid over an injured man. The blanket was large, and the woman stood up to shake it quickly to stretch it out. There was no sound from the material. She had been somewhere like this before. She didn't like it then, and didn't like it now.

Sarah stood up quickly, looking around the room. Her quick moves didn't draw anyone's attention besides Sisters Cecelia and Angelica, who were staring right at her. Sister Angelica stood next to Sarah, her mouth was still moving, but Sarah couldn't hear the constant prayer. Not that that hadn't happened before. It had become so much a fabric of her life, the sound of it had often blended into where she no longer noticed, but this wasn't one of those times. When she tried to hear it, it wasn't there. A parade of pin pricks moved up her spine.

A few others appeared to have taken notice of what was, or wasn't happening. They looked confused and scared, as they tried to talk to each other, but couldn't hear one another. If Sarah knew how to comfort them, it wouldn't make any difference, they wouldn't be able to hear her. A few became frantic and slammed their fist into the floor. There was no bang or thud from the impact, but it did vibrate the table they were close to, causing the light of the candle to flicker ever so slightly, spreading its light outward and into a darkened corner. It was during one of these flickers when Sarah saw it. A shadow whose source was not from the room. It was human, and not human. It stood upright on long muscular legs. Its torso towered up to the ceiling with long arms that dangled down. The face was just a shadow, no features. No eyes. No mouth.

Sarah watched the spot each time the light flickered back into the corner, hoping that her mind was messing with her under the strain of the day. No such luck. It was there each and every time, and it was moving. Each move of the flame showed it had moved several feet in. Its first stop was Lord Negiev, where it appeared to stop right on his chest. Lord Negiev gasped for air. Then there was the kick to Madame Styvia as it passed her. She rolled to the floor, clutching her ribs. Now it was in the light of all the candles and drew the attention of everyone in the room. Most let out silent screams. As it moved passed those screaming, they froze like some a statue in tribute to the horror they felt. Once far enough past, the silent screaming began again. Sarah felt its strange hold grabbing hold of her as it approached. First it was hard to move, then impossible as some invisible force squeezed her. It wasn't painful, but just enough to restrict her movement. Internally she struggled to move, but externally nothing moved.

The shadow leaned down over Father Lucian. It spoke in a deep thunderous voice, and Sarah could hear it. It appeared everyone else could too. The words were not ones she recognized. Powerless, she could only stand there and watched Father Lucian's head rise toward the creature. There was no struggle from the dying priest. All the fight in him had left hours ago. All he had left to offer was his last breath, which he exhaled as a white mist that the shadow appeared to breathe in and lean back to let it soak in.

Emotions flooded inside Sarah from everywhere. Her mentor, her confidant, the man that saved her life and kept her going was now dead at the hands of this beast. Her sorrow mourned his loss. Her sadness knew she would miss their talks. Her compassion worried if he felt pain in his last moments. Her rage wanted revenge. That was a new one. Rage was one emotion she had never felt before, not even as a disgruntled teenager. She had gotten angry a few times. Mad more than a few. She wanted blood this time, and the desire continued to boil inside of her. A finger moved, then a hand. The force that held her was still there, but it was loosening its hold on her. Her arm broke free and she thrust her hand at the shadow. All the rage inside her focused through her hand in a blinding light that sent the shadow flying back through and over people until it came to a stop.

Rage consumed her, and now her legs were free and moving on their own following the creature. It had sprung back up to its feet, looking straight at Sarah. Backing up a few steps it boomed, "You!" Then let out a scream of its own and vanished. Taking with it the veil of silence that had draped over the room. The screams that were silent now filled the room. There was crying and moaning. But one sound was missing. Father Lucian was now silent. There were no more raspy breaths. No rise and fall of his chest. He was gone.

12

"It was him!", Madame Styvia cried, still clutching her ribs.

With the return of sound, Sarah's calm returned, and the rage disappeared like fog burning off from her courtyard on a spring day. With it, a flood of questions replaced the dark and dangerous emotion. On top of the list was, "Why did he come here?"

"No!", Madame Styvia exclaimed, struggling to stand. The nurse who had been tending to her burnt hands tried to keep her seated on the ground, but Madame Styvia pushed against her until she was finally on her feet, forcing the woman to follow her up as she wrapped her hands. "I mean, yes. The shadow was behind it. But, what you did, it was him. That thing in you. I felt it as clear as I did that day in the woods," she declared. She paused. Confusion replaced the fear and anger that were both clear on her face. "And, IT was scared of him," she said, puzzled.

"Sister!", exclaimed Sister Genevieve as she ran across the room to Sarah. "I felt him too. That was him."

"That can't be," Madame Styvia questioned out loud. Sarah could see her mind fluttering around as though. It was probably the same thought Sarah had. Each time she or any of the other keepers went out there, they were sent running for their lives. They were no match for Ala and stood no chance of ever re-closing the seal. But her little friend Abaddon seemed to be something Ala wasn't too fond of. *Why?* Well, Sarah remembered there was a hierarchy to demons. A rank, so to speak, just as there is anywhere else in life. In its simplest view, we have the food chain that is based on survival abilities between hunters and preys. Militaries have a chain of command based on responsibility. The demon order is based on influence and ability. Or that is what Sarah remembered being taught by Father Lucian. He gave her a caveat, though. While he believed there was some order based on respect, and possibly fear, in that world, the order they had documented was created by man and should in no way be considered the rule of law. It was a good thing too. She didn't remember the specifics to know where either sat on that tree. The only true evidence she could go on is what she had just seen. Her little friend was higher than Ala.

"Can you control him?", Madame Styvia asked. She again was pushing away from the nurse who had finished wrapping one hand and was attempting to start on the other.

"Yes. No. I don't know," Sarah stammered wearily. Only a few times had she felt a little part of him influencing her and her ability, but that was far different from letting him out and giving him the wheel. She had never even let him out of the trunk before, and the sisters helped her keep both hands on the wheel and both feet on the pedals.

"She can," stated Sister Genevieve. "She has done it before. I have seen her."

"Yea, but not fully. I have let just a bit of him out here and there," protested Sarah. She looked at Madame Styvia, "And, only when absolutely necessary." She looked down at the lifeless body of her mentor and sighed remorsefully. "Father Lucian and one of the sisters have been with me to keep him from taking too much control each time." Her voice sounded almost as lifeless as Father Lucian was. Sarah knew where this was going, and it scared her to death. It meant to open up to what she had feared most since that day. Not just letting Abaddon's presence enhance her abilities, but truly letting him out. Could she hold on to the leash enough to pulling him back when she was ready? She had more than a few doubts.

13

How did I get talked into this?

Sarah had plenty of time to wonder that as she walked alone back out to the hill. There wasn't much debate about the idea. Sarah didn't even put up a protest; half expecting others to do that for her, but found herself surprised when they didn't. Were they so out of options that the threat of losing her to the demon within was... tolerable?

That thought made her sick to her stomach. This was basically a sacrifice. Send the possessed girl out to face certain death, and hope she can fix the seal before she is lost. Hollywood couldn't come up with a storyline like this. She would laugh, if she didn't feel so scared and, off. The fear was there, but there was something else she couldn't put her finger on. The thought it was him already bubbling up added to her fear and the uneasiness that had a hold on her. This was the first time in years she had been alone with her thoughts. All the time a sister was by her side praying, supporting her, comforting her. She had forgotten what it was like to truly be alone, and she didn't like it.

The ground rumbled around her, but not under her. The flames shooting up from the cracks in the ground in her path stopped. Even the sky above her looked less ominous, changing from a glowing red and black mixture of clouds and fire to grey with every step. Each step she moved deeper and deeper into the grey, feeling less of the world around her. Ahead of her, she saw the hill. She was close. Close enough to see the shadow figure standing on top. *Ala is out*, she thought to herself.

"Yes, he is. The seal of man is broken," said a familiar voice from inside her.

"Oh God," she croaked.

"No my child, God is not here," Abaddon said, and Sarah descended into the grey void.

"Our Father, who art in heaven...", she started. Her voice quivering and echoing in her own head.

"Relax. This is about Ala, not you at the moment."

Sarah felt him getting stronger. The sensation of her life draining away to nothing but a whisper while something else was in control, was one she hoped to never feel again, but here she was. A floating presence along for the ride. The world was just shadows that moved in and out of the static filled void. She could see the shape of the hill and another shape flying at them. It appeared to hit them and knock them to the ground, but she felt no pain. She didn't before either.

They leapt off the ground toward the shadow figure on the hill, covering a great distance and going over the top of Ala. Her hand reached out and scratched gouges into the shadow. Lightning flashed with each slash, and red streaks ran down from the wound as smoke rose from the gashes. It screamed. Her hand made another lightning accented slash from behind, producing another large rip in Ala's black scaley tissue, but they didn't get away unscathed. Its hand reached out and grabbed Sarah, Abaddon, by her long black hair and slung them across the landscape. When they landed, her hands scratched at the ground, trying to grab a hold of something. She finally latched hold of a boulder that had been heaved up by the earthquake, jerking them to a stop just in time. Her legs dangled over the edge of one of the huge cracks in between blasts of flames.

They got up just before the next shot of fire would have consumed them. The heat from the blast singed the ends of Sarah's hair that flowed behind her in the wind, but that didn't stop them. They rushed Ala again. Sarah could only watch as this time her body aimed low for the legs of the towering beast. They hit with a great force, sending the creature stumbling back. They continued to push, forcing it to slide back along the ground. Through the grey void Sarah saw what Abaddon was trying to do. There was a huge rip in the earth's surface at the top of the hill. That was where it was imprisoned. He was trying to put him back. If she could help push she would have, but instead was just along for the ride.

Closer and closer they pushed the creature who struggled for his balance. The flames that had started from the gashes on the top of its shoulder had now grown to cover most of its back. Even though Sarah couldn't hear its screams, she could see its pain. They were almost to the hole when Ala took notice as the back of its foot cleared the edge of the rupture. It grabbed them again by the hair and flipped them up and over its back and down the backside of the hill.

This isn't working, Sarah thought. Abaddon had started another attack. Again, focusing on the creature's legs. Ala was ready this time, hunched down in a power stance, legs bent, ready to take the impact. It swiped twice with its hands, contacting the second, swatting them away like a fly. The grey static shook with that impact, giving Sarah a clearer view of the world around them. Ala felt it had the upper hand and again was hurling rocks and chucks of dirt at them. With ninja like quickness, Abaddon dodged every rock, tree, and lump of dirt. Only a volley of iron crosses made it through, slashing at Sarah's skin. None of them were mortal wounds, and for that moment Sarah was appreciative for being in the blank void away from the pain.

Abaddon was slow to get back on his feet. The acts were taking a toll on a level Sarah couldn't understand. Each of these swipes, hits, and slashes were more than they appeared. This was not just two mortals fighting. These were immortals, and each attack delivered an impact from the ages. More of the world crept in as Ala stomped toward them. Looking larger than it had ever looked before.

"You're losing," Sarah exclaimed.

"Shut it. I know what I am doing," Abaddon's voice boomed in the world of static.

"So, you know you are losing," Sarah responded as they made another attack. This time with one of the crosses that Ala had thrown at them. Abaddon grabbed it and ran at the charging Ala, holding it like a spear. He didn't throw it and instead waited until he was on top of him to thrust it at any exposed body part of the creature. The black scaly flesh of Ala bent, but didn't break. The cross did, with a long metallic chink as it broke in two and fell to the ground. Sarah could only watch as the long black clawed hand of their adversary whacked them enough force to send them flying again. Before they even landed, she heard a deep laugh.

"So, you think we are losing?", Abaddon chuckled. "Watch this. I am the great deceiver, remember. I am playing with Ala."

They landed between two rips in the earth's crust. The fire that avoided them now roared up all around them. Through the grey void Sarah saw Ala standing tall. Almost... gloating. *You sick bastard*, was the thought in her head when Abaddon reached out with both of her hands and summoned the flames that roared around them. They leaned toward them and away from their source, towering hundreds of feet in the air, spinning like giant tornadoes. More flames joined them, then dirt, rock, remains of the trees that had been destroyed by the earthquake and Ala. It all mixed into a tower of molten death that was fired at Ala with alarming speed. Even in the void Sarah heard the impact as it exploded on contact, covering him in flames and burning debris, sending him stumbling backwards one step, then a second. The third step was what Abaddon waited for, and Sarah heard the cheer inside when the great creature fell back into the large hole it came from.

"Now I need your help," Abaddon said.

"What?", Sarah asked, surprised. What did he need from her?

"We can't die, and unless you want us to go on fighting forever, which is fine by me, you need to do something. I can't. That is not my thing, and you saw what happened when I tried to use that cross, it broke."

The yin and the yang, Sarah thought. They are chaos and she is order. It is up to her to restore order. Confused as to why Abaddon would give her this opening. Why not continue to fight and maybe enslave Ala? Not that she wanted to give him any ideas. It was an opening, and she had to take it. "Then you need to let me out and go back to your spot, don't you?"

"Nice try," he said with his evil laugh. Sarah hoped he would choke on that laugh one day, but she knew there wasn't a chance that would happen. "You get just a little. Just enough to do this." The static cleared more, and Sarah not only could see the world, but could also hear the groaning of the great beast coming from the hole, feel the ground still rumbling under her feet, smell the acidic and toxic sulfur filled fires all around them, and feel the pelting of rain. What she couldn't do is move her own feet. He was still in control of that.

Before Sarah left, Madame Styvia explained the rite to her. It seemed simple enough. Sprinkle some holy water on a series of crosses and plunge them into the ground while proclaiming, "With the power of almighty God, I lock this unclean spirit for all eternity." She will need to say it with each cross she plunges down. The anointing with oil was just something Madame Styvia did believing it would make it stronger. When Sarah asked how many she needed to put in the ground, Madame Styvia said, as many as you can.

"Well, Sister," Abaddon's voiced sizzled. "What are you waiting on?"

"I need my hands," she said.

"Okay."

She felt water droplets hitting her bare arms, stinging the cuts and scrapes she had suffered during the fight. Both hands reached up and grabbed the cross still hanging around her neck and recited, "Blessed are you, Lord, Almighty God, who deigned to bless us in Christ, the living water of our salvation, and to reform us interiorly, grant that we who are fortified by the sprinkling of or use of this water, the youth of the spirit being renewed by the power of the Holy Spirit, may walk always in newness of life." Then she raised her hands up, while reciting, "Lord give me the power to seal this beast. Allow me to use your symbols of the crucifixion to renew and restore our faith in you..." Every cross, broken and unbroken, rose up from the ground. They hung in the air as the rain fell and the lightning struck. Her hands directed them over to the hill where they had spent years standing guard, and with a single drop of her arms, all but one crashed into the ground with a mighty flash. The ground shook, but Abaddon kept Sarah standing. Around them cracks sealed, fire disappeared, and the great gouge that was the hill closed with the walkway leading up like a giant zipper, and looking like nothing had happened. Above them, the smoke from the fires cleared, allowing the first rays of sun in that day. It was late afternoon, and the rays just cleared the horizon, but they looked brilliant to Sarah as they hit the one cross that still hung in the air.

"Almost done," Sarah said."

"Almost?", asked Abaddon as the last cross turned and shot toward Sarah.

14

"I woke up nine days later in a hospital, all bandaged up. Most of the scars from that day are gone, with the exception of the one on my chest." Sarah told Ralph. "Mind you, I won't show that scar. I am rather modest about any exposures of the flesh. That scar and the anguish I feel for the loss of Father Lucian have stayed with me until this day."

"That's all right, Sister. How bad were the injuries?"

"Well," Sarah said as she recalled them in her mind. "Several dozen scratches and scrapes. Sorry, I can't remember the exact number anymore. A broken right femur that I was told happened during the struggle with Madame Styvia, Lord Negiev, and Sisters Cecelia and Angelica as they retook control, and three broken ribs and a collapsed lung from when I tried to take control."

"So, it was a battle to bring you back?", Ralph asked. With his hand, he signaled for Kenneth to zoom in tighter for this dramatic question.

"I was told it took three days. I don't remember any of it, and they never told me anything about it," She leaned forward. Her expression and tone turned serious. "You see, it is best not to tell someone what they did when they didn't have control. The guilt can be paralyzing and devastating. It is why to this day, I still don't know what happened there or at Miller's Crossing, and I have stopped asking." Her look and tone were a message that she hoped Ralph and Kenneth both understood. She looked at her brother, who was nodding his agreement to the message.

"I completely understand," Ralph said.

"The person's mental health is as important as their faith," Sarah added.

"I do have some follow-ups. Details, that I want to get right in my notes. Things that if I messed up in the documentary, we will be ridiculed about." Ralph said. He flipped to an empty page in his notepad and gripped the pencil at the ready to jot her answers down. "You mentioned the rite to relock the seal involved soaking the cross in holy water and then putting it into the ground. First, did you take a vial out there with you? Second, how many crosses did you actually do that with?"

"Why, all of them," Sarah said, answering the second question first.

"All of them?," Ralph asked, perplexed. The pencil remained still in his hand. "Weren't there thousands?"

"More than ten thousand, I believe, and I used them all."

Ralph's pencil made its trek back behind his ear as he looked on, confused. "Sister, how did you cover all ten thousand or more crosses in holy water so quick? Or did this really take days to do?"

"Ralph, I consecrated the rain, then drove all but one of them into the ground to relock the seal. The last one, I drove into my chest to try to take care of Abaddon, and myself. A move he hasn't forgiven me for yet. I only wished my aim was better. We would have avoided the dark days that were ahead."

Continue Reading...

The fourth book in the series, "Trial by Faith" will be released early in 2022. You can go ahead and preorder it now and save 50% on the retail price.

[Preorder the "Trial by Faith"](#)

Sarah Meyer has lived a rather interesting life. Conjoined with a Demon that won't let go, she has been under the protective custody of the Sisters of San Francesco. Under the guidance of her mentor, Father Lucian, she helps solve some of the world's most terrifying paranormal mysteries. These are her stories.

Sarah did the unforgivable in Lithuania, she let the demon out, and even though it was the only way to stop a bigger catastrophe, she faces scrutiny, and a trial by a counsel of Cardinals at the Vatican. If she is found guilty of unholy acts, she will lose her place at the convent she has called home for over a decade, and live the rest of her life in physical shackles and spiritual pain. She remains resolute that she did the right thing, but Vatican law is black and white, and without her mentor Father Lucian to stand up for her, she needs a savior.

Have you read the whole Miller's Crossing series?

Miller's Crossing Book 1 – The Ghosts of Miller's Crossing
Amazon US
Amazon UK

Ghosts and demons openly wander around the small town of Miller's Crossing. Over 250 years ago, the Vatican assigned a family to be this town's "keeper" to protect the realm of the living from their "visitors". There is just one problem. Edward Meyer doesn't know that is his family, yet.

Tragedy struck Edward twice. The first robbed him of his childhood and the truth behind who and what he is. The second, cost him his wife, sending him back to Miller's Crossing to start over with his two children.

What he finds when he returns is anything but what he expected. He is thrust into a world that is shocking and mysterious, while also answering and great many questions. With the help of two old friends, he rediscovers who and what he is, but he also discovers another truth, a dark truth. The truth behind the very tragedy that took so much from him. Edward faces a choice. Stay, and take his place in what destiny had planned for him,or run, leaving it and his family's legacy behind.

Miller's Crossing Book 2 – The Demon of Miller's Crossing
Amazon US
Amazon UK

The people of Miller's Crossing believed the worst of the "Dark Period" they had suffered through was behind them, and life had returned to normal. Or, as normal as life can be in a place where it is normal to see ghosts walking around. What they didn't know was the evil entity that tormented them was merely lying in wait.

After a period of thirty dark years, Miller's Crossing had now enjoyed eight years of peace and calm, allowing the scars of the past to heal. What no one realizes is under the surface the evil entity that caused their pain and suffering is just waiting to rip those wounds open again. Its instrument for destruction will be an unexpected, familiar, and powerful force in the community.

Miller's Crossing Book 3 – The Exorcism of Miller's Crossing – Available Fall 2020
Amazon US
Amazon UK

The "Dark Period" the people of Miller's Crossing suffered through before was nothing compared to life as a hostage to a malevolent demon that is after revenge. Worst of all, those assigned to protect them from such evils are not only helpless, but they are tools in the creatures plan. Extreme measures will be needed, but at what cost.

The rest of the "keepers" from the remaining 6 paranormal places in the world are called in to help free the people of Miller's Crossing from a demon that has exacted its revenge on the very family assigned to protect them. Action must be taken to avoid losing the town, and allowing the world of the dead to roam free to take over the dominion of the living. This demon took Edward's parents from him while he was a child. What will it take now?

Miller's Crossing - Prequel – The Origins of Miller's Crossing
Amazon US
Amazon UK

There are six known places in the world that are more "paranormal" than anywhere else. The Vatican has taken care to assign "sensitives" and "keepers" to each of those to protect the realm of the living from the realm of the dead. With the colonization of the New World, a seventh location has been found, and time for a new recruit.

William Miller is a simple farmer in the 18th century coastal town of St. Margaret's Hope Scotland. His life is ordinary and mundane, mostly. He does possess one unique skill. He sees ghosts.

A chance discovery of his special ability exposes him to an organization that needs people like him. An offer is made, he can stay an ordinary farmer, or come to the Vatican for training to join a league of "sensitives" and "keepers" to watch over and care for the areas where the realm of the living and the dead interaction. Will he turn it down, or will he accept and prove he has what it takes to become one of the true legends of their order? It is a decision that can't be made lightly, as there is a cost to pay for generations to come.

WHAT DID YOU THINK OF THE STORIES OF SISTER SARAH?

First of all, thank you for purchasing The Stories of Sister Sarah: Crossed. I know you could have picked any number of books to read, but you picked this book and for that I am extremely grateful.

I hope that it provided you a few moments of enjoyment. If so, it would be really nice if you could share this book with your friends and family by posting to [Facebook](#) and [Twitter](#).

If you enjoyed this book and found some benefit in reading this, I'd like to hear from you and hope that you could take some time to post a review on Amazon. Your feedback and support will help this author to greatly improve his writing craft for future projects and make this book even better.

You can follow this link to [The Stories of Sister Sarah: Crossed](#) now.

ALSO BY DAVID CLARK

Want more frights?

Ghost Storm – Available Now

Amazon US

Amazon UK

There is nothing natural about this hurricane. An evil shaman unleashes a super-storm powered by an ancient Amazon spirit to enslave to humanity. Can one man realize what is important in time to protect his family from this danger?

Successful attorney Jim Preston hates living in his late father's shadow. Eager to leave his stress behind and validate his hard work, he takes his family on a lavish Florida vacation. But his plan turns to dust when a malicious shaman summons a hurricane of soul-stealing spirits.

Though his skeptical lawyer mind disbelieves at first, Jim can't ignore the warnings when the violent wraiths forge a path of destruction. But after numerous unsuccessful escape attempts, his only hope of protecting his wife and children is to confront an ancient demonic force head-on… or become its prisoner.

Can Jim prove he's worth more than a fancy house or car and stop a brutal spectral horde from killing everything he holds dear?

Have you read them all?

Game Master Series

Book One - Game Master – Game On

This fast-paced adrenaline filled series follows Robert Deluiz and his friends behind the veil of 1's and 0's and into the underbelly of the online universe where they are trapped as pawns in a sadistic game show for their very lives. Lose a challenge, and you die a horrible death to the cheers and profit of the viewers. Win them all, and you are changed forever.

Can Robert out play, outsmart, and outlast his friends to survive and be crowned Game Master?

Buy book one, Game Master: Game On and see if you have what it takes to be the Game Master.

Available now on Amazon and Kindle Unlimited

Book Two - Game Master – Playing for Keeps

The fast-paced horror for Robert and his new wife, Amy, continue. They think they have the game mastered when new players enter with their own set of rules, and they have no intention of playing fair. Motivated by anger and money, the root of all evil, these individuals devise a plan a for the Robert and his friends to repay them. The price… is their lives.

Game Master Play On is a fast-paced sequel ripped from today's headlines. If you like thriller stories with a touch of realism and a stunning twist that goes back to the origins of the Game Master show itself, then you will love this entry in David Clark's dark web trilogy, Game Master.

Buy book two, Game Master: Playing for Keeps to find out if the SanSquad survives.

Available now on Amazon and Kindle Unlimited

Book Three - Game Master – Reboot

With one of their own in danger, Robert and Doug reach out to a few of the games earliest players to mount a rescue. During their efforts, Robert finds himself immersed in a Cold War battle to save their friend. Their adversary… an ex-KGB super spy, now turned arms dealer, who is considered one of the most dangerous men walking the planet. Will the skills Robert has learned playing the game help him in this real world raid? There is no trick CGI or trap doors here, the threats are all real.

Buy book three, Game Master: Reboot to read the thrilling conclusion of the Game Master series.

Available now on Amazon and Kindle Unlimited

Highway 666 Series

Book One – Highway 666

A collection of four tales straight from the depths of hell itself. These four tales will take you on a high-speed chase down Highway 666, rip your heart out, burn you in a hell, and then leave you feeling lonely and cold at the end.

Stories Include:

- Highway 666 - The fate of three teenagers hooked into a demonic ride-share.
- Till Death – A new spin on the wedding vows
- Demon Apocalypse - It is the end of days, but not how the Bible described it.
- Eternal Journey - A young girl is forever condemned to her last walk, her journey will never end

Available now on Amazon and Kindle Unlimited

Book Two – The Splurge

A collection of short stories that follows one family through a dysfunctional Holiday Season that makes the Griswold's look like a Norman Rockwell painting.

Stories included:

- Trick or Treat – The annual neighborhood Halloween decorating contest is taken a bit too far and elicits some unwilling volunteers.
- Family Dinner – When your immediate family abandons you on Thanksgiving, what do you do? Well, you dig down deep on the family tree.
- The Splurge – This is a "Purge" parody focused around the First Black Friday Sale.
- Christmas Eve Nightmare – The family finds more than a Yule log in the fireplace on Christmas Eve

Available now on Amazon and Kindle Unlimited

The Stories of Sister Sarah: Ghost Island Copyright © 2021 by David Clark. All Rights Reserved.

All rights reserved. No part of this book may be reproduced in any form or by any electronic or mechanical means including information storage and retrieval systems, without permission in writing from the author. The only exception is by a reviewer, who may quote short excerpts in a review.

Cover designed by Eye Creation

This book is a work of fiction. Names, characters, places, and incidents either are products of the author's imagination or are used fictitiously. Any resemblance to actual persons, living or dead, events, or locales is entirely coincidental.

David Clark
Visit my website at www.authordavidclark.com

Printed in the United States of America

First Printing: May 2021

Printed in Great Britain
by Amazon